P9-DED-927

Louise
the Lily
Fairy

For Lily Bisseker, with lots of love

Special thanks to Sue Mongredien

If you purchased this book without a cover, you should be aware
that this book is stolen property. It was reported as "unsold and
destroyed" to the publisher, and neither the author nor the
publisher has received any payment for this "stripped book."

No part of this work may be reproduced, stored in a retrieval system,
or transmitted in any form or by any means, electronic, mechanical,
photocopying, recording, or otherwise, without written permission
of the publisher. For information regarding permission, write to
Rainbow Magic Limited c/o HIT Entertainment,
830 South Greenville Avenue, Allen, TX 75002-3320.

ISBN-10: 0-545-07092-9
ISBN-13: 978-0-545-07092-8

Copyright © 2007 by Rainbow Magic Limited.

All rights reserved. Published by Scholastic Inc., 557 Broadway,
New York, NY 10012, by arrangement with Rainbow Magic Limited.

SCHOLASTIC, LITTLE APPLE, and associated logos are
trademarks and/or registered trademarks of Scholastic Inc.
RAINBOW MAGIC is a trademark of Rainbow Magic Limited.
Reg. U.S. Patent & Trademark Office and other countries.

12 11 10 9 8 7 6 5 4 3 2 1   9 10 11 12 13/0

Printed in the U.S.A.

First Scholastic Printing, February 2009

Louise
the Lily
Fairy

by Daisy Meadows

SCHOLASTIC INC.

New York   Toronto   London   Auckland   Sydney
Mexico City   New Delhi   Hong Kong   Buenos Aires

The
Fairyland
Palace

Blossom
Hall

Fairy Garden

Leafley Village

Visitors' Centre

I need the magic petals' powers,
To give my castle garden flowers.
I plan to use my magic well
To work against the fairies' spell.

From my wand ice magic flies,
Frosty bolts through fairy skies.
This is the crafty spell I weave
To bring the petals back to me.

Contents

Woodland Walk

"Blossom Lake, this way!" Rachel
Walker called out, seeing the wooden
sign ahead. Buttons, her dog, trotted by
her side. He sniffed at the trees and
bushes along the way.

Kirsty Tate smiled at her best friend,
Rachel. The girls were taking a nature
walk with their parents. Buttons started

to speed up as they turned onto the trail, heading deep into the woods. Kirsty was so glad they were all spending spring break together this year. It made her think about when she first met Rachel. The two families had stayed next door to each other one summer on Rainspell Island. Since then, Kirsty and Rachel had become best friends — and they always had the most exciting adventures whenever they were together!

Now the two families were staying at Blossom Hall, an old mansion, for a whole week. Today they'd planned to visit Blossom Lake.

"I can't wait to see the lake," Kirsty said, as she, Rachel, and Buttons led the way down a sloping path through the trees. "There was a picture in Mom's guidebook, and it looked really pretty."

Rachel grinned at Kirsty. "I wonder

what else we'll see today," she said quietly.

Kirsty knew exactly what her friend meant. "Oh, I really hope we meet another Petal Fairy," she whispered. "But remember what the fairy queen  always says — we have to wait for the magic to come to us!"

Kirsty and Rachel shared a wonderful secret. They were friends with the fairies! They'd had all kinds of fairy adventures together, and just two days before, they'd started a whole new adventure. This time, they were helping the seven Petal Fairies.

"Ah, there's the lake," said Kirsty's
mom, making the girls jump. Both Kirsty
and Rachel had been so busy thinking
about fairies that they hadn't realized
they were coming out of the forest.
There, ahead of them, was a stretch of
blue water with sunlight sparkling on its
surface.

They stepped out
into the sunshine
near the water's
edge. "It's
beautiful!" Rachel
sighed happily,
gazing at the woods
that surrounded the
water. "Is that an island in
the middle?"

"It certainly looks like one," her dad

said, shielding his eyes from the sun as he looked where Rachel was pointing. "Now don't go scaring the ducks, Buttons!" he said, quickly catching the excited dog's collar.

Buttons was rushing toward the ducks that were wading in the weeds at the side of the lake. "I think I'd better put you on a leash," Mr. Walker added, clipping it on to Buttons's collar.

"Oh, look!" Kirsty said excitedly. A small dock at the edge of the lake had caught her eye. It was a little farther along the path from where they were standing. There was a small wooden boathouse next to it, along with a few rowboats tied to wooden poles. Kirsty turned to Rachel, her eyes shining. "Do you want to take a boat out?"

"Can we, Mom?" Rachel asked, gazing hopefully at her parents.

The four adults looked at one another.
"I don't see why not," Mrs. Walker
replied. "As long as you can borrow
life jackets. You two can rent a
boat while we take a stroll around
the lake."

"Great!" Kirsty cheered. "Come on,
Rachel!"

Mrs. Tate took the girls over to the
 boathouse, where a
friendly man untied
a boat for them
and showed them
how to put on
their life jackets.
"Please be
careful, girls,"
Mrs. Tate said.

"Don't worry," Rachel replied, sitting carefully on the wooden seat. She felt a thrill go through her as the boat bobbed gently on the water. "We'll be fine."

"Thanks, Mom. See you later!" Kirsty called.

"Happy sailing," replied Mrs. Tate. She gave them a wave and went off with the other adults.

"So, who's going to row?" the boatman asked.

"We'll take turns," Rachel said. "Do you want to go first, Kirsty?"

Kirsty nodded happily. The boatman passed her a pair of oars, and helped slide them into the oarlocks.

"Thanks," Kirsty said, looking excitedly across the lake. There were lots of plants floating in clumps on the surface of the water, and she used an oar to pull one closer to her. The leaves of the plant were round and shiny. "Are these lily pads?" she asked the boatman curiously.

He nodded. "That's how Blossom Lake got its name," he said. "Because so many lilies blossom here. They're usually out by now, since this is such a warm and sunny spot, but they're late this year." His weather-beaten face creased into a smile. "You'll have to come back and see them when they're in full bloom," he told the girls. "It's quite a sight!"

The boatman pushed the rowboat out onto the lake, and the girls glanced at each other. "We know why the lilies

 aren't blossoming," Rachel said quietly, once they were out of earshot. "It's because Louise the Lily Fairy's magic petal is still missing!"

Kirsty nodded as she pulled on the oars. On the first day of their vacation, the girls had met Tia the Tulip Fairy. She had told them that the Petal Fairies' seven magical petals were all lost in the human world. Mischievous Jack Frost had sent his sneaky goblins to steal the petals, so he could use their special magic to make flowers grow around his freezing ice castle. But when the Petal Fairies had used some of their own magic to rescue the petals, it had mixed with Jack Frost's spell to cause a

huge explosion — sending the petals spinning right out of Fairyland! Without their magic petals, the Petal Fairies were unable to help the flowers grow and bloom, so it wasn't just the lilies that were late to bloom this year. None of the flowers were growing properly! The girls had vowed to help the fairies find their petals and return them to Fairyland. They had already found Tia's tulip petal and Pippa's poppy petal, which meant that some flowers were starting to bloom brightly again, but five magic petals were still lost.

Rachel smiled across the boat at Kirsty.

"Are you thinking what I'm thinking?" she asked.

Kirsty grinned. "I'm thinking that I hope we find the lily petal today!" she replied.

Island Surprise

Blossom Lake really is pretty, Rachel thought as Kirsty rowed farther into the center. The water was shimmering in the sunlight, and emerald-green dragonflies skimmed across its surface. Every few moments, Rachel saw a couple of big orange fish dart from one side of the boat to the other.

"We're getting close to the island,"
Kirsty said after a little while. "Should
we go over and explore it?"

Rachel turned around in her seat and
saw the island looming up behind her.
There was a small wooden dock there,
and she could see trees and shrubs a
little ways up the shore. "Good idea,"
she said.

Kirsty steered them toward the dock.
They tied the boat up carefully and
climbed out.

"What a nice place!" Rachel said,
gazing around.

Kirsty agreed. Butterflies fluttered
between the trees, and birds were
singing. "Come on, let's explore!"
she said.

The two girls set off on a stone path
that led away from the water, through
the trees. They hadn't gone very far
when they heard a noise. *Pssst!*

"What was that?" Kirsty
whispered, stopping
and looking around.

Rachel grinned.
"Over there," she
said. She pointed
at a nearby shrub,
and then she waved
at it.

Kirsty stared in surprise.
Why was Rachel waving at a bush?
Then she giggled as she spotted the tiny
fairy who was peeking out from between
the leaves. Kirsty and Rachel had met all
the Petal Fairies on the first day of their

vacation, and she recognized who it was
at once.

"Hello, Louise!" she said, as she and
Rachel hurried over. "We were hoping
we'd see you again today."

The fairy beamed
and flew up into the
air in a burst of pale
pink sparkles.
"Hello there," she
said cheerfully. "I
was hoping to see you, too."

Louise had blond hair
that fell to her shoulders in
curls. The sides were pinned back
with pretty pink hair clips. She wore a
pale green dress with a light pink silk
sash and light green boots that matched
her dress.

She landed lightly on Rachel's shoulder, and her pretty face clouded over for a second. "Have you seen the goblins yet? They're on the island, too. I just heard them saying that they know where my petal is!"

Kirsty frowned at the news. She never liked running into Jack Frost's goblins, but this time it was even worse. Jack Frost was so desperate to get his hands on the magical petals that he had given his goblins a wand full of his own icy magic. Kirsty and Rachel had always been able to outwit the goblins in the past, but it was much harder

now that they were armed with a
magic wand!

"What does your petal look like?"
Rachel asked.

"It's pale pink," Louise told her. "It
helps all the lilies in the world to grow,
and all the other light pink flowers, too."

The girls had learned that each magic
petal was responsible for making its own
particular type of flower grow. It also
helped other flowers that were the same
color as the petal to bloom.

"Where are the
goblins?" Kirsty
wanted to know.

"They're on the
other side of the
island," Louise replied.

"Follow me!" She fluttered her glittery wings and took off into the air. Rachel and Kirsty followed her through the trees. Both girls were nervous about the goblins. Kirsty hoped they would be able to find Louise's lily petal before one of the goblins spotted it!

After a few minutes, Louise perched on a large bush and motioned for the girls to crouch behind it. Then she put a finger to her lips. "Don't make a sound," she whispered, waving her wand.

24

A flood of pale pink fairy dust billowed out from the wand's tip. At once, the twigs and leaves of the bush parted, making a neat peephole for Rachel and Kirsty to see through. The girls could see that they were now all the way on the other side of the island. The blue water of the lake was only a few steps from their hiding place, and Rachel's eyes widened as she saw a bridge joining the island to the far shore of the lake. She hadn't noticed that before. Then she realized that it wasn't an ordinary bridge. It was made of ice!

"The goblins used Jack Frost's wand to create the bridge," Louise confirmed in a tiny whisper.  "That's how they got across to the island in the first place." Kirsty couldn't help staring at the icy bridge. It looked beautiful with the sun shining on it, making the ice crystals glitter and twinkle. But as she watched, she realized that the bridge was dripping. "It's melting!" she gasped.

Splash! A section of the bridge collapsed into the lake.

Louise nodded. "It certainly is," she said. "They'll have to use their magic to make another bridge if they want to get off the island again."

Rachel was frowning. "What are the goblins doing?" she asked in a low voice.

The girls and Louise stared at the strange sight. One of the goblins was up in a tree that stood on the edge of the island. The tree's branches reached out over the water. The goblin was dangling upside down from a branch by his huge

green feet. Underneath
him swung six other
goblins. They were
hanging, one after
another, each
holding on to the
feet of the goblin
below. The goblin
at the bottom of
the chain, who had
particularly large
ears, had his arms
stretched out. He

seemed to be trying to reach something
on the surface of the lake, but the girls
couldn't see what it was.

Just then, he turned around to yell
instructions to the others. Kirsty and

Rachel gasped as they saw exactly what he'd been trying to reach.

Louise's pale pink lily petal was right there on a lily pad, just a fingertip away from the big-eared goblin's grasp. And as the girls watched, the wind sent the lily pad sailing even closer to him. The friends held their breath. Any moment now, the goblin was going to turn back and see that the lily petal was right under his nose!

Splash and Grab

"Don't touch that petal!" Rachel yelled, charging out from the girls' hiding place. Kirsty and Louise were close behind her.

The goblins were startled by the appearance of the girls. The one holding the big-eared goblin's feet let go of him in surprise, and there was a huge splash as he fell into the lake.

Kirsty, Rachel, and Louise couldn't help laughing as he staggered out of the water, dripping wet. He shook himself like a dog, sending water and clumps of weeds flying everywhere. His friends, who were still hanging from the tree, roared with laughter.

But the wet goblin didn't seem to mind his friends' amusement. He was too busy waving the pink petal in the air, with a look of triumph. "Look what I've got!" he bragged. "And I'm going to deliver it to Jack Frost personally. Boy, is he going to be happy with me!"

Louise stomped her foot in dismay, sending a little puff of pale pink sparkles floating up into the air. "Oh no," she wailed. "I can't believe he has my lily petal!"

The other goblins scrambled down from the tree. "Let us look at it!" called a squinty-eyed goblin who was holding Jack Frost's magic wand.

But the big-eared goblin proudly clutched the petal to his chest. "No way," he retorted. "I'm taking care of this myself!"

"That petal belongs to Louise the Lily Fairy," Kirsty said, in her fiercest voice. "Now give it back!"

"No!" the big-eared goblin sneered. He dodged out of the way as Rachel tried to grab him.

"Run for it!" ordered the goblin
with the wand. At his words, all
seven goblins rushed past the girls at
top speed.

Kirsty, Rachel, and Louise chased them
through the trees, and back to the other
side of the island. It wasn't long before
the goblins reached the dock. Rachel and
Kirsty heard cries of glee as the goblins
spotted the girls' rowboat.

"Just what we needed!" one cheered.

"And the bridge is melting, so those rotten girls will be trapped!" snickered a second one.

Rachel stared in horror as she approached the dock and saw the goblins grouped around the little boat.

"Hey, that's ours!" she yelled, but the goblins were already hopping aboard, waving to the girls.

"Too late!" the big-eared goblin declared, as one of his friends untied the rope and quickly pushed the boat away from the island.

"Bye-bye!" cackled the goblin with the wand. He clutched his sides as if it was the funniest thing ever.

Kirsty and Rachel could only stand and watch them go from the edge of the dock. "Oh no," groaned Kirsty. "Without our boat, we're stuck here. What are we going to do?"

A Wave
of Panic

"I'm going to turn you into fairies, of
course," Louise said with a playful smile.
She waved her wand over the girls, and a
fountain of lily-scented fairy dust swirled
all around them. Instantly, Kirsty and
Rachel felt themselves shrinking down to
fairy-size.

Rachel fluttered her delicate wings and

glared at the goblins. "What are
we waiting for?" she cried. "Follow
that boat!"

The three fairies flitted across the water
toward the rowboat. Kirsty could see that
the goblins weren't going very fast, and
as she flew closer to the boat, she realized
why — the goblins could never do
anything without arguing!

"I should be captain!" the goblin with

the petal yelled. "I have the magic petal."

"No, I should be," the squinty-eyed goblin argued. "I have the wand!"

The goblin with the petal scowled and jumped to his feet. The boat started to rock from side to side, dangerously close to tipping over.

"Hey!"

"Sit down!"

"Stop it!" his friends shouted in alarm, pulling him back down.

"You call yourself a captain? You nearly dumped us all in the water, you fool!" one of them complained.

"So I'll be captain, then," the squinty-eyed goblin insisted.

"Then I'll row," announced a skinny goblin. "No, I want to!" protested the tall goblin next to him. "You can have one oar each!" snapped the squinty-eyed goblin, bossily. "Those are the captain's orders, and you're not allowed to argue!"

The fairies hovered behind the boat as the two goblins began rowing. Unfortunately, they moved their oars in different directions, and the little boat didn't move at all.

The squinty-eyed goblin sighed. "Useless!" he complained. "You have to row at the same time, and in the same direction! Fools!"

At long last, the rowers seemed to get the hang of it and the boat slowly moved away across the lake.

"I wonder where they're heading," Rachel said thoughtfully. "It would be too risky for them to go back to the dock near the boathouse, wouldn't it? What if the boatman spotted them?"

Kirsty narrowed her eyes as she noticed the boat veering off in a different direction. "Look," she said, pointing to a spot on the shore. It wasn't too far from the boathouse. "There's a beach there, and it's hidden by trees. I bet that's where they're going. Let's fly ahead and wait for them there."

The other two
nodded, and they
all flew to the
small stretch of
beach. They
landed on the sand.
As the boat came closer,
Louise waved her wand and turned
Rachel and Kirsty back into girls.

"What took you so long?" Rachel
asked the goblins, smiling, as the boat
approached the shore.

The big-eared
goblin groaned
when he saw her
standing there.
"Oh, not you
again!" he said,
making a face.

The goblin with the wand grinned. "Don't worry, I can take care of them," he boasted. He pointed the wand at the girls and shouted, "Magic, make a great big wave, to wash those pesky girls . . . away-ve!"

" 'Away-ve'?" Kirsty said with a snort. "That's a terrible rhyme!"

"They're not getting any better at making up spells," Rachel agreed.

"But that doesn't stop them from

working!" Louise cried in alarm. For there, rolling out of the sea toward them, was the most enormous wave they had ever seen. It looked like a huge wall of water!

Rachel and Kirsty started to back away, but they couldn't move fast enough.

"It's coming too quickly," Rachel gasped. "Help!"

47

Lost and Found

Louise reacted in a split second, throwing fairy dust over the girls. In the twinkling of an eye, they had turned into fairies again and were able to zoom high into the air. They were safely out of reach of the wave.

"Phew," Rachel sighed. "Thanks, Louise. That wave is huge!"

"And it's just about to hit the goblins," Kirsty said. "Look!"

The three fairies all peered down at the lake. The goblins were on the verge of getting caught in their own spell! They were all still in their boat, shouting and pointing as the magic wave drew nearer.

The wave rushed at them, picking up the boat and tipping it over. It swept the boat onto the beach and left it there,

upside down. Then the water receded
into the lake.

"Hey!"

"It's all dark!"

"Who turned the lights out?" cried
one of the goblins who was trapped
underneath the boat.

Next, there was a loud banging and
thumping sound. The three fairy friends
looked at one another, wondering what
to do.

"Those goblins should give that wand back to Jack Frost," Kirsty said.

"It's gotten them into big trouble this time!" Rachel agreed.

Louise nodded. "They're lucky that I'm nice enough to take pity on them!" she said, swooping toward the boat with Rachel and Kirsty flying after her.

Louise muttered a few magic words
and twirled her wand over the boat. Pale
pink glittery magic streamed from her
wand, and then the rowboat slowly
turned over so it was right side up on
the sand.

The goblins got to their feet, coughing,
sputtering, and shaking water off
themselves.

"I'm soaked," one muttered, making an angry face. "Dumb boat, dumb wave. And where's that petal, anyway?"

The goblin who'd been holding on to the petal looked upset. "It got washed out of my hands by that wave." He moaned, searching around for the petal. Then, not seeing it anywhere, he turned on the goblin with the wand. "It's all your fault!" he snapped. "You and your crazy spell!"

"My crazy spell?" the goblin with the wand replied. "Your crazy fingers, you mean. You should have held on to the petal a little tighter! I knew we should never have trusted you to look after it!"

As the goblins argued about whose fault it was, something caught Rachel's eye. She fluttered over the water for a closer look, then motioned to her friends.

"I've found the petal!" she whispered with a bright smile. "Look! There it is, floating on the lake!"

Lovely Lilies

Rachel swooped down to pick up the petal, but it was wet and heavy, so her friends flew to help.

A groan went up from the goblins on the beach when they saw what was happening. "Those awful fairies are going to get the petal now!" the big-eared goblin complained, stomping his foot in rage.

The squinty-eyed goblin lifted the wand high into the air. "Don't worry," he announced. "I'll take care of —" But the other goblins jumped on him before he could say another word.

"NOOOO!" they all cried together, as the girls laughed.

"No more spells! Look what happened the last time!" the skinny goblin complained, still shaking water from his ears.

Louise waved her wand over the lily petal, shrinking it down to its Fairyland size with a happy smile on her face. Then, holding on to it tightly, she flew back to the goblins. "Next time, don't take things that don't belong to you!" she scolded them. "And you can tell Jack Frost that, too!"

The goblins ignored her and stomped off with grumpy faces.

Louise hugged the girls gratefully. "Thanks so much, girls," she said. "Now I'd better take my petal straight back to Fairyland, where it belongs."

She pointed her wand at the girls and a cloud of fairy dust whirled around them.

All of a sudden, Rachel and Kirsty were their normal size again. They were sitting in the rowboat, with the oars in place!

Louise smiled. "I'll just get you back onto the lake," she said, with another wave of her wand.

Rachel and Kirsty grinned in delight as the boat slid gently down the beach and back into the water, all on its own.

"Thanks, Louise!" Kirsty called.

Rachel waved to the little fairy and then took hold of the oars. "Bye!" she said, blinking as Louise vanished in a puff of pale pink sparkles.

Rachel rowed the boat across the lake toward the boathouse. Luckily, Louise's fairy magic had completely dried the little boat, so

the boatman would have no idea
that one of his rowboats had
been tossed upside down
in a giant wave.

"Perfect timing,"
Kirsty said
happily as they
approached the
boathouse.
"Look — there
are our
parents."
Rachel turned
to see the four
adults strolling
toward the boathouse,
just finishing their walk.
"I bet we've had a more

exciting time than they have!"
She grinned.
"I bet . . . oh!" Rachel
exclaimed in surprise
as she saw a single
pink water lily
unfold on a
lily pad nearby.
"The lilies
are blooming!"
she cheered.
"There's a
white one,"
Kirsty said,
pointing. "Oh, and
another pink one.
They're all opening!"
The two friends smiled at

each other. "Louise's petal magic is working again," Rachel declared. "That was quick!"

It was wonderful rowing back through all the beautiful pink and white lilies.

When the girls reached the boathouse, the boatman was shaking his head in amazement.

"And I was saying you'd have to come back to see the lilies in full bloom," he

chuckled. "It's almost magical the way they've all started opening up now!"

The girls nodded, but Kirsty didn't dare look at Rachel in case she burst out laughing. *Almost magical? It* was *magical!* she thought with a smile.

"Hello!" called Mr. and Mrs. Walker, striding up with Buttons alongside them.

"Did you have a good time?" asked Kirsty's dad.

Rachel looked at Kirsty. "Oh, yes," she said, grinning. "We had a *fairy* good time!"

RAINBOW magic™

THE PETAL FAIRIES

Now Louise the Lily Fairy has
her magic petal back. Next, Rachel
and Kirsty must help

Charlotte

the Sunflower Fairy!

Take a look at their next adventure
in this special sneak peek!

Village Visit

"*Welcome to Leafley,*" Rachel Walker read out loud as she and her best friend, Kirsty Tate, stopped at the message board outside the Visitors' Center. "*Come and see our beautiful village and our early-blooming sunflowers!*"

"Isn't Leafley a wonderful name for a village?" Kirsty laughed, as she and

Rachel waited for their parents to catch up with them. The Tates and the Walkers — and Rachel's dog, Buttons — were spending spring break together at the Blossom Hall hotel, which was close to the little village of Leafley.

"You kind of expect a place called Leafley to be full of beautiful flowers."

Rachel nodded, and then looked serious. "But will the Leafley sunflowers be blooming at all, now that the Petal Fairies' magic petals are missing?" she asked.

Kirsty frowned. "Good question. We haven't found Charlotte the Sunflower Fairy's petal yet!" she exclaimed.

If you love Rainbow Magic, you'll love Sparkle World Magazine!

Special Introductory Offer
5 issues for
$19.97

(Regular subscription price $24.97)
Canadian subscription $24.97
(includes postage)

Join us for lots of magical fun in Sparkle World!

To subscribe call
1-800-444-3412
(Quote code J8PT/Sparkle World.)
or visit
www.redan.com
Join Rainbow Magic and other much-loved characters in this sparkly girls' magazine, full of early-learning fun!
Each issue has an activity workbook, stories, crafts and more!

www.rainbowmagiconline.com   © 2008 Rainbow Magic Limited

There's magic in every book!

The Rainbow Fairies
Books #1–7

The Weather Fairies
Books #1–7

The Jewel Fairies
Books #1–7

The Pet Fairies
Books #1–7

The Fun Day Fairies
Books #1–7

SCHOLASTIC and associated logos are trademarks and/or registered trademarks of Scholastic Inc. ©2008 Rainbow Magic Limited. Rainbow Magic is a trademark of Rainbow Magic Limited. Reg. U.S. Pat. & TM off. and other countries. HIT and the HIT logo are trademarks of HIT Entertainment Limited.

SCHOLASTIC

www.scholastic.com
www.rainbowmagiconline.com

HIT entertainment

FAIRY3